P9-CSW-003

A VOTE IS A POWERFUL THING

Catherine Stier

illustrated by
Courtney Dawson

Albert Whitman & Company
Chicago, Illinois

To those with the courage and commitment
to change the world for the better—CS

To my mom. Thank you for teaching me
my voice matters.—CD

Library of Congress Cataloging-in-Publication data is on file with
the publisher.
Text copyright © 2020 by Catherine Stier
Illustrations copyright © 2020 by Albert Whitman & Company
Illustrations by Courtney Dawson
First published in the United States of America
in 2020 by Albert Whitman & Company
ISBN 978-0-8075-8498-9 (hardcover)
ISBN 978-0-8075-8499-6 (ebook)
Printed in China

10 9 8 7 6 5 4 3 2 1 RRD 24 23 22 21 20

Design by Valerie Hernández

For more information about Albert Whitman & Company,
visit our website at www.albertwhitman.com.

A vote is a powerful thing.
That's what my teacher says.
Powerful enough to change the world.
That gets my attention. So I listen up.

"One vote, combined with other votes during an election, is what puts our mayors, governors, senators, and even the president of the United States into office," Ms. Trask explains.

Right now, that's what everyone's talking about—the presidential election in November.

But Ms. Trask says we'll soon have our very own classroom election too.
"It's for something I think you'll all care about," Ms. Trask hints.
"Elections can be about important issues as well."

A vote, we find out in class, really *is* a powerful thing.
So powerful that throughout our country's history, people organized, marched, and protested for the right to vote.

Voting Rights Act 1965

My grandma knows a vote is a powerful thing too. Powerful enough that she's up early this Saturday.

"Please vote for funds to save the wilderness park," Grandma tells every grown-up she meets. "Being outside in the forest is good for you! And where else in this town can folks experience the wonders of nature?"

People don't know much about the wilderness park.
I do.
It's where I saw my first mountain laurel in full bloom, my first
turtle in a pond, my first swallowtail butterfly. It's where I spotted my
first and only great horned owl. I want to save the park too. But I don't
know how to help.

At school, we talk more about voting. We learn that supporters of a candidate or a cause may spend lots of time and money on campaigns with signs, ads, and speeches. They do this in hopes of winning each citizen's one precious and powerful vote.

That day, Ms. Trask makes her big announcement:
"Our classroom election will be for...our next field trip! You may
choose between the cookie factory or the wilderness park."

"The cookie factory tour gives free samples. Yum!" says Lynn.
"I heard there's a nature trail at the park," says Reed.
"What's so special about that?" asks Ginny.
Suddenly, I know this election *is* important to me.
And I have an idea.

Some of my classmates have never been to the wilderness park. If they saw it just once, I know they'd want to visit again. And bring their families. Then maybe lots of people would care about saving the park.

"Ms. Trask," I say, "I'd like to campaign in support of the wilderness park."

"An inspiring idea, Callie," she says.

So first, I design posters.
I draw postcards.
I write a speech. It isn't easy.
"Maybe you could share your best memories
of the park, Callie," Dad suggests.

So that's what I do.
But I'm not the only one campaigning.

On our class's election day, Lynn makes her speech first. She's read all about the cookie factory. She tells everyone we could learn important things on the tour about food and science and technology.

She isn't wrong. The cookie factory *would* be a good field trip.

"And don't forget—free cookies," Lynn says.

Then it's my turn. First, I tell everyone about my best wilderness park memories—the woodsy forest smells, the cardinals singing in the trees, and the tadpoles with long tails and brand new legs wriggling around the pond. And that awesome owl!

And like Lynn, I've done my research too.

"Scientists believe that spending time in nature can help kids be healthier and smarter and more creative," I say. "And even kinder too."

"Really?" Ginny asks.

"Uh-huh. But we can all find out for ourselves," I say. "Vote for the wilderness park!"

Everyone in class receives a paper ballot. One by one, we cast our votes.

I hold my breath as Ms. Trask counts them up. She pulls the last ballot from the box and holds it up.

"I am proud of Lynn and Callie," says Ms. Trask. "You both ran great campaigns and made some excellent points about each field trip. So excellent, in fact, that the election is tied now, with just one vote left to count."

Ms. Trask unfolds the last
ballot and smiles.
"And the winner is..."

At the wilderness park, Reed scrambles up a rock. Diego sniffs a wildflower. Ginny examines a spider's web through a magnifying glass.

And then we all spot it—a quick flash of red as a fox darts from a bush and dashes across the path.

I've never seen a fox before.

"That's amazing," Lynn whispers. "I wish my brother could see all this."

"And my mom," says Reed.

I'm full of hope.

Because now
I know it's really true...

**A vote is a
powerful thing.**

★ ALL ABOUT VOTING ★

Every election has a ballot—a list of choices for voters. When we as citizens vote, we choose our leaders: we decide who will be the president of our nation, and who will be the governors and mayors and other officers of our states and towns. We vote to choose our representatives in Congress and state legislatures, our judges (in some states), and other public servants. We also vote to decide on new laws or rules in our communities, and sometimes we even vote on how our local governments spend money. Voting is a right, but it's also a responsibility. Our votes shape the future.

Our nation's biggest election, to elect the president, vice president, and other federal officials, takes place every four years in November, on the first Tuesday following the first Monday of the month. This November day is also designated for electing members of Congress. Members of the House of Representatives are elected every two years, while senators are elected every six years. Many state and local governments have elections on this day too, but they can hold elections at other times of the year.

Who Can Vote?

To vote in an election in the United States, a person must:
- be a US citizen.
- be eighteen years old by the date of the election.
- meet the voting requirements of the state in which they live.

US citizens living in US territories cannot vote for president in the general election. Other voting eligibility rules vary by state.

How Do Citizens Vote?

We often think of voting as something that happens only on election days and at polling places—designated places with voting booths—but there are several ways citizens can cast their ballots, depending on the rules in the states where they live.

Early voting: This option offers citizens the chance to vote before Election Day at special polling places. In some states, early voting takes place a few days before Election Day, in other states it can be several weeks.

Voting by mail: A few states use this method as their primary voting system for major elections. Ballots are sent to voters many weeks in advance, and they must be received or postmarked by Election Day.

Voting by absentee ballot: This is another form of voting by mail available to voters if they are unable or (in some states) choose not to vote at their polling place in person. Members of the military and other citizens who are overseas on Election Day vote by absentee ballot. The state of Texas allows its NASA astronaut residents to cast absentee votes from space!

Voting on Election Day at a polling place: People visit specially assigned places near their homes to vote. Polling places are often set up in public spaces, like schools, libraries, or even firehouses. In some communities, people use voting machines or computer touchscreens to vote; in other places they might use paper ballots or fill out forms. Voters are allowed to vote in booths with partitions or curtains for privacy.

Voting Rights in the United States

When the United States was founded, voting was usually restricted to white men who owned property. Since then, amendments to the Constitution, acts of Congress, and challenges to unfair laws have removed barriers to voting and granted voting rights to more citizens. Here's a timeline of some key events in our country's voting history:

- **1870** The Fifteenth Amendment to the Constitution grants men the right to vote regardless of race, color, or former enslavement. But discriminatory laws in many states still keep African Americans from voting.

- **1920** The Nineteenth Amendment gives women the right to vote.

- **1924** An act of Congress grants Native Americans citizenship and voting rights, though many Native Americans, especially those living on reservations, remain unable to vote under state laws for many more years.

- **1948** Miguel Trujillo, a Native American and World War II veteran, wins a legal challenge to a New Mexico law that barred him from voting.

- **1964** The Twenty-Fourth Amendment outlaws poll taxes for federal elections.

- **1965** The Voting Rights Act bans local poll taxes, poll tests, and other unfair obstacles that had been used to deny African Americans and other groups the right to vote.

- **1971** Thanks to the Twenty-Sixth Amendment, the minimum voting age for all citizens is lowered from twenty-one in some states to eighteen throughout the US.

- **1990** The Americans with Disabilities Act includes rules to ensure that people with disabilities have access to polling places and equal opportunities to vote.

Callie and the Wilderness Park Campaign

Callie and her grandmother care deeply about their local wilderness park, and in the election in this story, voters in their town will decide whether or not to give the park money to help it stay open. This kind of decision is often called a ballot measure or proposition—a question on an election ballot about something that affects the community. Callie and her grandmother want voters to vote yes on helping fund the wilderness park, so they hope to convince people that the wilderness park is good for individuals and the town.

See Further Reading for resources Callie might have used in her classroom campaign.

Further Reading

Websites about Elections, Voting, and Government

Who can and can't vote in US Elections:
https://www.usa.gov/who-can-vote
Ben's Guide to the US Government:
https://bensguide.gpo.gov
iCivics, civics learning and games:
https://www.icivics.org

Books for Young Readers

Shamir, Ruby. *What's the Big Deal about Elections.* New York: Philomel, 2018.

Stier, Catherine. *If I Ran for President.* Chicago: Albert Whitman, 2007.

Winter, Jonah. *Lillian's Right to Vote: A Celebration of the Voting Rights Act of 1965.*
    New York: Schwartz & Wade, 2015.

Callie's Wilderness Park Resources

The National Wildlife Federation:
https://www.nwf.org
The National Park Service:
https://www.nps.gov